Horace Henway
Brushes It Off

For Andrew and Kate.

Copyright © 2019 by Kathleen Arthur
All rights reserved.
Published by Hillsboro House Books
Tucson, AZ www.hillsborohousebooks.com

ISBN: 978-1-7333512-0-1

Library of Congress Control Number: 2019912588

This book is printed with soy-based ink. The artwork is acrylic on stretched canvas and was critiqued by my daughter, Kate.
Printed in China
First Edition

HORACE HENWAY
Brushes It Off

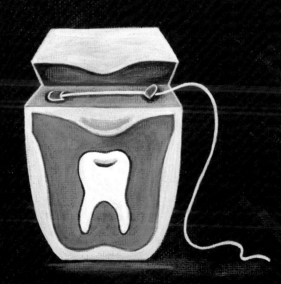

Kathleen Arthur ● Hillsboro House Books

I'm just a regular kid.
My name is Horace Henway.
Today I did a favor
for a friend who's old and gray.

He lives across the street,
and goes by Mr. Hunt.
He loses things a lot.
He'll tell you that upfront.

His house is very cluttered.
I've heard it called a pigsty.
He lives there by himself
with an old black cat named Sly.

One day he lost his toaster,
and I found it in his chair.

Today he lost his teeth
in all his stuff somewhere.

"Young Horace," he explained,
"I admit my mistakes.
I neglected my teeth,
and now I wear fakes.

My real teeth rotted
from too much decay.

I didn't brush it off,
and they withered away.

If I don't find my fakes,
I'll chew with my gums.
But if that doesn't cut it,
I'll have to eat crumbs.

This morning when I woke,
they were gone from this jar.
I've looked all around.
They COULDN'T be far!"

I said, "Don't worry, Mr. Hunt.
It may take me a while.
But I'll look in every
place, in every heap,
and every pile."

So I looked in all the rooms
and behind all the doors,

from the tops of the ceilings,

to the bottoms of the floors.

I even checked the fish bowl
while the hungry cat stared,
but the only thing I found
was a fish swimming scared.

I searched between the seats
of his old pickup truck,

and in his rusty mailbox
without a turn of luck.
I was about to give up
and call it a day,

when the old cat, Sly,
started walking my way.
He rubbed against my legs ...

and looked up with a grin.
That cat KNEW all along
where the teeth had been!

And now I, Horace Henway,
make a promise to myself
to take care of my teeth
as a part of good health.

I'll go to the dentist
and take their advice.
Every day I will floss
and brush at least twice.

So my teeth will be real
and stay right where they're at,

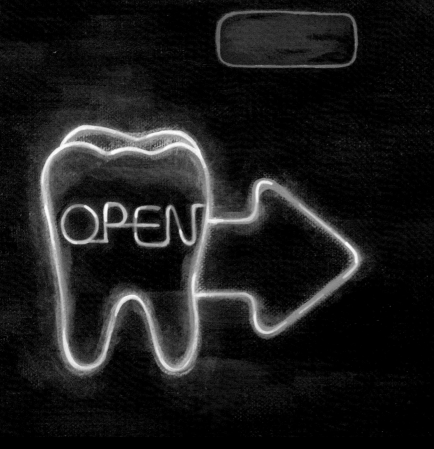

not kept in a jar ...

or worn by a cat.